REDRUM

I0542871

Ferropolis
Originally published in German as *Kalte Berechnung* by
dotbooks Verlag; 1 edition (July 4, 2012).
ISBN 978-3-943835-15-1
Copyright © 2012
(First American edition)
Copyright © 2019
REDRUM BOOKS, Berlin
Publisher: Michael Merhi
Translated by Stefanie Maucher
Editor (American edition): Greg F. Gifune
Cover design and concept:
MIMO GRAPHICS by using an
illustration by Shutterstock.

ISBN 978-3-95957-561-4

E-Mail: merhi@gmx.net
www.redrum-verlag.de

YouTube: Michael Merhi Books
Facebook: REDRUM BOOKS
Facebook Group:
REDRUM BOOKS—Nichts für Pussys!

Stefanie Maucher
FERROPOLIS

The Book:

They meet on the Internet, a young teenage girl and an older man who at first seems kind and friendly. He thinks he's found the perfect victim. He thinks he can control her. He thinks he can manipulate and threaten her into doing any number of unspeakable things, not only online but in person. What he doesn't know is who he's actually talking to, and what lies in wait at their real-life meeting.

An abused child ... A monstrous sexual predator ...a mother bent on revenge ... and a storm of violence and intrigue where the lines between predator and prey no longer exist.

This is FERROPOLIS.

Prey for mercy.

The Author:

Hard, suspenseful and often far too realistic ... Stefanie Maucher's stories crawl under her readers' skin. Born in Stuttgart in 1976, the author loves to take a look into the deepest and darkest human abysses and relentlessly talk about what she finds there.

The mother of two now lives in Eastern Germany, where she works as a proofreader and translator whenever she's not writing her own books.

Table of content

Stefanie Maucher

FERROPOLIS

Thriller

Chapter 1

I walk alone, but I'm part of a group. Freaks like me, on their way to Ferropolis – the City of Iron. My feet stick in my jump boots, and I've squeezed myself into a pair of unusually narrow jeans. My footfalls, ordinarily accompanied by the melodic click of high heels, sound slow and unfamiliar. My hair bounces on my shoulders, blazing red and irritating me. I wipe it out of my face again and again so I can see. I look straight ahead. I'm not looking for company. Not yet. The rest of my presentation is owed to the occasion as well: My top isn't a belly shirt but shows off enough to allow a glimpse of my piercing every now and then. Broken off Mercedes-stars adorn my rebellious arms. Worn trophies combined with real handcuffs, the silver contrasting with my black velvet, elbow-length gloves. Instead of a belt, long leather straps serve as a fixture for my trousers, laxly knotted at the side.

As cervical jewelry, I'm wearing a dog-collar, with sharp and dangerous looking spikes. A small key is attached to the ring, where a pet owner normally hooks the dog leash. Is this my sick way of peddling the key to my heart? Who knows?

My makeup gives me the appearance of a woman in her early twenties. I have the typical look of a sixteen-year-old girl pretending to be older than she is. Indefinable.

I carry a cell in the right pocket of my pants. Less a phone and rather a modern substitute to replace the Walkman which I dragged around constantly when I was a kid. A cable leads to an earplug; music roars from the small speaker, makes me inaccessible to the outside world. A few notes and a small amount of coins can be found in the left trouser pocket. The ticket for today's open air concert in Ferropolis, the city of steel, is in the back pocket. Now and then I feel for it nervously, afraid I might lose it. Without it I won't meet my date.

I wonder if you are as excited as I am. We became acquainted on the Internet. Today we'll be able to look into each other's eyes for real, for the first time. I'm sure you'll meet my expectations, but will it be the same for you? Self-doubt is normal for most, especially teenagers, but my fear is different.

You found me on Facebook. One of those friendship-requests of a foreign person, accepted without shyness or further thinking about it, followed by the usual small talk. *How are you? What's up?* Compliments quickly followed. You were so interested and showed such a winning personality; finally, everything started to make sense. The phenomenon that it's sometimes easier to talk with a stranger than to share our secrets with people we know created a feeling of closeness between us faster than might've normally been the case.

Checking my virtual mailbox became thrilling. People once wrote love letters, but today it is emails. Holding hands and kissing has been replaced with showing your nipples during a video chat, and all at once you become intimate with each other, even though it all takes place in the alleged security of cyberspace. Nevertheless, this intimacy feels real. It means something, awakens feelings, even if one can't touch the other.

Your touch, I ask myself, how is it going to feel? How will it be, to stand in front of you, face to face, and feel your hands on my skin? How do you smell? I know, something will happen today, for the first time - my first time. Ahead lays a road I've never walked before, but one I unquestionably want to travel. I hope I won't be too nervous. Maybe it will excite me. I will look you in the eye, enjoy the moment ... Although I long for this moment, I'm afraid your touch might burn me, change me irreversibly and mark me permanently, like a branding iron. I'm sure, that our meeting will somehow change you as well. This day can pass none of us without leaving a trace. Something of me will remain in you. Our fortunes are intertwined.

Reluctantly, I shake my head, try to edge out these thoughts and to focus on my steps. My boots are new, their weight unfamiliar. They cost my gait its usual elegance, but give the impression that I might be cool and determined no matter what happens. The external impression is deceptive, just a facade. I feel as if I'm dancing along the edge of a sleeping volcano, purposely crushing the thinnest layers of crust and afraid the whole thing might awaken and erupt at any moment. I try to mask my nerves, but my right hand gives me away, kneading on a yellow anti-stress ball with a smiley face on it I bought at a toy store the day before.

Vibrations from my right pocket interrupt my thoughts. I stop walking, switch the ball to my other hand, pull out my cell and read the text message that just came in:

Are you there yet? Short and tight. No kiss? I bundle off an answer quickly:

Not yet. Are you already waiting for me?

I let my eyes wander over the swelling river of people that flow to the concert, watching for yours in the mass of faces passing by. It seems as if we've been waiting forever to meet. All at once, Einstein's theory of relativity becomes plausible to me: time stretches noticeably. I turn the music louder, before I put the cell back in my pocket and set myself into motion again. While passing by, I scrutinize the small groups resting at the side of the street; swarms of colorful birds of paradise - flamboyant personalities, whose hairspray-glued plumage can withstand the heaviest winds. I pass them slowly.

The Gremminer Lake, which surrounds the peninsula Ferropolis, extends on both sides of the road. This rises from the former desert, which the opencast mining Golpa North has left, before it has been flooded artificially. Now, because no more brown coal is mined, they facilitate the overexploitation in the purses of attracted tourists. The steel giants living on the peninsula are seen from afar, between whom the stage and the concession stands take place; an imposing sight.

While I let myself float in the anonymous mass, further in the direction of the entrance, the gigantic bucket-wheel excavator with the nickname *Big Wheel,* a bit farther away, catches my eye and puts me under its spell. That's where we want to meet. You told me when and where you want to have me; I had to get the ticket myself. To the sound of my favorite band I will lose the rest of my innocence; in front of this impressive backdrop that you chose especially for this occasion. For days I can barely think of anything else. I chomp at the bit, exactly as you do, getting ready for it, and wait for that moment to come.

I gather my hair as if by rote, and throw it back as I so often did when it was longer, but it's only medium length now, and it falls back immediately, provocatively cascading across my naked shoulders. Yesterday I cut off my long black hair, crying and yet hungry to fulfill your vision of me. I bleached the remaining hair and then colored it. I will do anything just to get close to you. You know exactly what kind of girls you desire. You described your expectations explicitly. Your way of demanding things, uncompromising and assertive, makes it easier to fulfill your wishes. You know what you want, seem so self-confident, dominant and challenging. I know it should scare me. It does, but at the same time it arouses the bad girl in me. Yes, I want to play – with you! If adjustments are needed, and my now deep red hair is your fetish, then I'm willing to give you what you need in order to get what I want. You think I'm impressionable, a bit naive, but my thoughts and urges are not child-like at all.

Earlier, just as you demanded, I took out my cell and shot a picture of me and my new haircut in front of an old wagon that now is part of this industrial museum. With the former mining train, another attraction for tourists, I could cover a part of the trip, at which end I'm supposed to lose my purity. I sent you this picture as proof that I'm truly on my way and did what you've told me prior. As a confirmation that I'll turn up for the date and that I behaved well.

I have waited for your answer a long time,hoping to avoid that critical look I fear. Until the news finally came that our meeting will take place. Today, you will come.

I know you wrote *come* with a filthy undertone. Because I act like you require, you stopped thinking with your brain. I already know you better than you realize.

Chapter 2

I stand waiting in line. The air, weighted with perfume, smoke and deodorant, rests like an invisible thick skin over this lindworm of people, sweating and too close together. All that is putting my patience to the test and fuels my nervousness. I approach the entrance. There I pull out my ticket and pass the security check. A stocky woman in a bomber jacket searches my almost painfully pushed up breasts, and for a moment I hold my breath, as her hands carelessly frisk my boots and glide up my legs. Finally I empty my trouser pockets in front of her, lay their contents and even my anti-stress ball in a small plastic tub which she's holding. A few seconds later, after she's examined everything, I pick up my stuff and wait while she tears off a corner of my ticket and finally allows me to pass.

I enter the event location, float with the mass and swim within the flow of people, before I let myself drift to the shore flooded with camping toilets. There I wait again till one of the stinking toilets empties. Inside, I check my make-up while breathing through my mouth and standing in a heap of urine-soaked toilet paper. The mirror is smeared with graffiti informing me that someone named Mandy is a bitch and probably has gonorrhea or worse. I put my right boot on the already muddy toilet seat and loosen the bootlace. Even after countless exercises at home it's not easy: I must maintain a strong stand in my boots and nevertheless be able to grab in with the level hand.

The guitarist in the opening act causes the first feedback of the evening, while a girl waiting on the other side starts to hammer on the hard plastic door which separates me from the outside world. It looks like she's in a hurry. I tear open the door and squeeze myself past her into the open with an audacious *"don't pee in your pants"*. There I consume a deep breath of fresh air before I push and shove my way to the concession stands and order a coke. I'd prefer something harder, but of course I don't want any discussion about my age. We won't meet - you made that perfectly clear - before the main act starts to play. You'll wait for me offside, where nobody else will be. Till then the dusk gives way to night, so that we remain unseen, away from the floodlight, on the dark side of the

Big Wheel. There will be only us, even when there are 20 000 other people around.

I put the plastic mug to my lips and drink eagerly. While I take a big gulp, my cell starts to vibrate in my pants. I choke. A cold flood runs along my chin. I quickly catch the drops before they can reach my neckline and leave an ugly stain on my top. Before I pull the cell and read your message I wipe my wet hand on my jeans.

Where are you now?

Why are you speeding it up? Do you want to meet me by now, before I consider this whole thing differently during the waiting period? Are you afraid I could back down? I look around. There are many good viewpoints. An uncomfortable thought occurs to me. My red hair stands out even in this mass of people. Maybe you can find and observe me even if I don' tell you exactly where I am. Just because I can't see you yet doesn't mean you can't—or haven't—seen me.

My place is right beneath the *Mosquito,* a gigantic Caterpillar wheel extractor. A few steps lead up to the mighty monster of steel, which looks nothing like the tiny insect for which it's named.

There I squeeze myself through, move upwards and stand in the shade of the immense bucket chain that juts out above the steps. Here my red hair will shine less like a signal fire, and I have a better overall view of the area. So I take my cell and pass the position of the concession stand, which I can see perfectly from here. While my eyes glide over the people beneath me, looking for a newcomer who's obviously on the search too, my thoughts wander.

The feelings you release in me are indescribable. They blaze in me like a fire that's consuming everything, a fire that can only be extinguished with your blood. The message I sent you earlier comes to mind again. The one with the picture you liked so much. I remember the relief I felt when your answer finally arrived. I felt relieved because you, so little like in our previous chats, have no idea that you're no longer dealing with the fourteen-year-old girl you originally met, months before you and I had first contact. It happened shortly after her birthday. Her gift from her loving grandfather was her own laptop. She'll chat with classmates, watch videos on YouTube, innocent fun, I thought, so why not? I thought it would be safe, that she'd be fine, so I handed the laptop over to her without giving it much thought.

No, you haven't talked to my daughter, whose naivety you have used for a long time now. Not since I found out what you did. You persuaded her to get undressed in front of her webcam and in front of you. She was a child who had no experience handling predators like you, even if she looked mature for her age. You couldn't anticipate that this child has a mother with astonishingly youthful features. Friends often say it would be easier to believe we were sisters, rather than mother and daughter. I look a decade younger than I actually am and with the right make-up I still look like a minor, trying to get into a nightclub. The new hairstyle supports the impression. Obviously you agree. Otherwise you would have been suspicious or disappeared into the same cyberspace from which you came.

Maybe I wouldn't be so furiously angry, if you had at least left the child alone. She'd been eager to try new things, but she lost the desire to play with you pretty quickly. After the first time, she wanted to stop your conversations. For her they were not erotic at all. The childish romantic feelings, caused by your flattery and manipulative compliments, quickly lost their appeal. Soon as she gave you what you were looking for it became clear her naked body was all you'd ever been interested in. Apparently you thought she wouldn't figure this out, that you'd done enough preliminary work to keep her in your clutches. But it started to strike her that the whole thing was about you, not her. It was about your satisfaction, your desires and needs, not hers. And she finally realized she was being used. This wasn't her first love because love had nothing to do with it. So she began to be coy, to invent excuses to try and distance herself from you.

Of course it had struck me that my already quiet child became even quieter. She backtracked more and more and appeared to be heavy-hearted. Whenever I questioned her or asked what was wrong she always said, "It's nothing." I've already heard it too often during my life and every time it turned out to be a lie.

"It's nothing" was what my own mother said every time she claimed to have tripped or bumped into something. As if she somehow believed I was unable to hear the fights she and my father had. They were so loud I could hear them in my room or even on the other side of the garden fence. Everybody knew why my mother wore long-sleeved sweaters in summer, and often wore sunglasses even if it was getting dark out. I remember the looks from the neighbors, and how they'd look at her with compassion but never say a word. Yet they all knew. And I knew too. I knew exactly what had happened behind those closed doors. Ours was a home that only appeared safe from the outside.

But that kind of deflection disturbed me even more when it came to my daughter.

Of course I tried to talk to her and let her know she could and should come to me with any problem. But I didn't force my fourteen-year-old, who was already wrestling with shame and fear, to tell me what was really happening. I tried to be a loving, open-minded and progressive mother. I didn't hit her or strong arm her, but instead did my best to respect her privacy.

Which is why I felt so guilty when I crept into her room and searched her things for the first time.

I found nothing that would help me in any way, so I left her private kingdom with no answers and a guilty conscience. Some days later, still driven by vague unrest and doubts, I searched her computer. There I found the log files, the transcripts of your conversations. My daughter didn't know yet how one deletes temporary data or a chat history. With every line I read I developed a deep-rooted, implacable hatred. When I finished reading I had to vomit. I thought you were a perverted pig. Since then I've come to learn you're much worse.

In the log files I read that my daughter told you she couldn't turn on the camera because her younger sister always came into her room and bothered her. You then asked how old her sister was, if she'd already grown breasts too and how big they were. Pretending you were joking, you suggested she should tell her little sister come and join the two of you, that it would be fun. That would have been *it*, right? The lucky shot, like winning the jackpot in a lottery. Fortunately the risk that the little one might tell on you kept you from insisting. Finally, you had nothing to hold against her that would have secured her silence. But you didn't accept the *"No"* to more cam-chats with you, coming from the bigger one. You started threatening her, you would publish very intimate pictures, screenshots you've made without her knowledge during your chats. "The principal of your school," you said, "will certainly be happy if I send him those images. And your classmates will surely like them too." You have blackmailed her, put her under pressure and made her appear in front of the cam, even more intimately than before.

All this I knew when I sat down at the edge of her bed that evening and started the most difficult conversation I'd ever had with my daughter. We talked a long time, and the harder she cried the more my hatred for you grew. I have held her in my arms and told her she hasn't done anything wrong. That she was just too inexperienced and trusting and that she must not be ashamed. I let her know that somebody who acts like you did is criminal, despicable and ill. I said you deserved to be punished and I'd make sure you were. This promise conjured something on her pretty face, for the first time in weeks, which was nicer than any smile: Hope.

The next day I went to the police and asked what one can do about someone like you. The answer was frustrating: Even if they found out who you are, you would hardly get more than a monetary penalty. The sentence, that could be expected, would be much harder if you had contacted her a few days before her fourteenth birthday or if my even younger daughter had really joined in. However, I could file an "announcement because of sexual insults against an unknown person"- at most. And they told me, that the criminal prosecutions often fail because of the fact that the perpetrator is able to camouflage his paths on the worldwide net. Nowadays no pedophile, so they said, would be so silly that he wouldn't veil his IP address by a proxy server. The most frightening information though, was that my daughter would have to make a statement at the police station herself, despite the evidence on the computer, and later she possibly would be subpoenaed in court. I thought about how tough it was for her to talk about it, even with me, and I recognized how bad it would be for her to tell this story in front of strangers. Besides, what if the press picked up the story and it followed her around for the rest of her life?

I refused to name you. But I had not forgotten my promise.

In the evening I logged in to her accounts.

It didn't take long until a message from you popped up. The play began. I answered. Pretty quickly, after some small talk, you asked if I'd be alone. When I said yes you came right to the point. You told me you were so horny and that you wanted to see me. I lied, and told you my cam was broken. It wouldn't work anymore since my dumb sister played something on my computer without even asking permission. Later I even covered the lens with thick tape and we started a few fruitless attempts which brought you nothing but a black picture. You were stumped for an answer and couldn't find out which technical issue caused that error. Apparently you have believed my lie.

We talked a long while and I did my best to seem naïve, adapting my language and using the slang and expressions kids use today. I tried to get information about you and failed over and over again because you have remained unflustered with the subject *you and your cock*. You made it clear how hard you were while thinking of my daughter's body, and how good it felt to touch yourself while thinking of her. It seemed to be important to you, that I said things that confirmed your masculinity. You absolutely wanted to hear how great you are, and how it would work me up, how much I'd love to feel you deep inside me. You asked for that over and over again. I gave it to you, graphically, but it disgusted me. Only the knowledge that these talks had a deeper purpose made them bearable at all. *What doesn't kill you, makes you stronger,* I thought, while I forced myself to excite you.

My father used to say that a lot. With a shrug, concisely, always when someone shed a tear because of him. Every time I howled because he slapped me for no apparent reason or if my mother could hardly walk because he had beaten her so badly. In her case he was wrong: My mother did not become strong. The contrary was the case. Something in her was broken by his cruelty. There was an expression one generally only witnessed in zoo animals, in the eyes of captive gorillas, for example, for whom freedom is only a faded memory from a life they of long ago. I swore to myself no one would ever find that kind of hopelessness in my eyes, and long ago promised myself I would be strong, to never allow anyone to humiliate me or strip me of my dignity and pride. But I degraded myself, didn't I, when I joined you in your games? Broke my promise while giving you whatever you wanted. And when you got in front of your cam and jerked off, did you really imagine I found that attractive? Do you think it got me wet? If you'd been able to see yourself through my eyes you would've been so horrified you would've likely taken your own life.

All those subsequent nights I put up with your perversions in the hopes you might disclose something that would reveal your identity, your address, a place I could send someone to beat a conscience into you. I have endured your disgusting imagination, suffered through the gossip and stories and even the horrible sight of you masturbating. Besides, I had the feeling I couldn't gain ground. Although I got to know more of you, it was hardly useful. I prayed for a chance, even one break. Why, for God's sake, couldn't your camera simply fall down and land on a piece of paper with your address, or offer even the slightest clue as to who you were? A naive thought, yes, but one I had again and again.

The frustration in you seemed to grow as well. You became restless. Again you started threatening. It wasn't enough for you to simply describe the things you wanted me to see, or those things you wanted me to show you. The failure of my webcam became more and more of a problem, at least for you, and you complained how it was against our agreement. Of course you also had a solution. There was something I had to do for you, only once, and then you'd leave me alone. What it turned out to be, revealed to me who you really are and gave me goosebumps.

Chapter 3

My thoughts are interrupted abruptly, because my look firmly fixes on a man who looks around, obviously searching for something. It has become so dim in the meantime that I must narrow my eyes to see well. The hair color fits. The size could be also right. He's standing exactly where you'd expect me to be. "Damn it," I think, wishing your online profile picture wasn't so small and indistinct. Is this you? My heart beats faster. But then a young woman approaches the man. She falls into his arms, wraps hers around his neck and gives him a long lasting kiss. No, this isn't you.

Where are you? It feels as if an eternity has passed since I sent you the last message. I stare at the cell, awaiting further news. Finally, after several minutes that feel like hours, it vibrates and a new message appears.

Meet me at half past nine at the Big Wheel, clocklike.

No greetings, no kisses, no more smooth, flattering talk, just clear and concise instructions. Quickly, I close the message and take a look at the watch on the display. It reveals that I still have more than an hour. I put the cell away.

Looking up again, I see you.

You're standing absolutely still in the mass of people, maybe fifteen feet from the steps, and staring at me. My pulse races again. Terrified, I stand up and accidently knock the mug down the stairs. I try to go unnoticed, but I'm afraid you've seen me and my instinctive attempts to creep deeper into the shade. I remain frozen, like a deer in headlights, unsure of how to react. This is not the right place or time, and not how I planned things.

Meanwhile you're sure that I've discovered you too. You smile at me and smoothly wave your hand. What do I do if you simply decide to approach me? For a moment I feel less like a hunter and more like prey that has run directly into a trap. I consider running to the other side of this steel giant, taking the steps and vanishing into the crowd. But will I be safe in the crush of people?

Or should I just do it here?

But then you turn around and disappear into the mass yourself. My gaze follows you, and the tension in me eases. Without letting you out of my sight, I run down the stairs, throw myself into the scrum and fight my way after you. For a short time I manage to follow you, tracking the backside of the head I think is yours. But again and again I'm standing in front of a living wall of flesh, finding no gap to slip through. I use my elbows to fight my way through, annoying several others who are upset with me for being so rough. But after some minutes you become a needle lost in this haystack of dancing people. I run in circles, trying my best to find you, but I become disoriented, and finally, give up. It becomes too hot, too oppressive in the midst of the countless strangers. At the same time these jeans get too tight and stick to me like a second skin. A claustrophobic feeling overcomes me even though I'm under an open sky. The meddlesome perspirations of the bystanders are taking my breath. The dog-collar constricts my throat and I can't breathe. The guy to my left scrutinizes me critically. Faintly, as if spoken from a great distance, his voice reaches me. "Hey, are you okay?"

For a split second I lose my equilibrium and I nearly fall. As the stranger reaches for my elbow I stumble away from him, answering with a shake of my head. I force myself to breathe. No, nothing's okay, absolutely nothing. But I don't want help. Need none. He shrugs and turns back to the stage. I'm looking for a fixed point at the edge of the crowd, the biggest and mightiest of the five exhibited excavators, and struggle through the crowd to reach this resting-point. The closer I get the better I feel. My breathing returns to normal and I slowly regain my composure and the ability to think clearly again.

I'm not surprised that you avoid a direct meeting at this point too. The brief intermezzo only served to reveal to you that I really am here. Maybe it was just a taste, a quick look at your prey, a kind of foreplay for you. But what you want requires a solitary place and the cover only darkness can offer. After all, it will prevent anyone else from seeing what you planned to do to a child, and above all, what you plan to do afterwards. Or will that come first? No, I think you'll do it last, so you can enjoy your power and the helplessness of your victim to the fullest.

Your suggestion has been that you and my daughter should meet here, so she could give you something you shouldn't even dream about. Her virginity is supposed to be the price to protect her from being named and shamed in public by you. Then you came up with this little request, which I'm sure you thought appeared harmless compared to the rest of your demands. That detail revealed who you really are. Nobody knows your name or your face, but you're still famous. Your crimes got you quite the reputation.

Chapter 4

This chain of murders dominated the news a year ago. They found six bodies, all young girls between twelve and sixteen, naked, first raped, then strangled, maybe the other way around. Crimes, committed with inconceivable cruelty. The culprit disposed of the corpses in lakes and rivers. Four of the bodies were found in a lake in Brandenburg. Although they had been weighted down, the gas bloating the bodies caused them to rise to the surface and float in plain sight. Two more were found in the *Mulde,* close to the position where that river disembogues into the *Elbe,* washed ashore by the annual high water. No one knows if there are more bodies, although an extensive search was conducted, using divers that covered a wide area. Media reports and the impatience of the public put a great deal of pressure on the investigators, but the police were no closer to apprehending the culprit. Many newspapers and reports took things too far, sensationalizing the crimes with lurid theories and inappropriate photos of the victims, one gazette even taking it so far as to publish a photo of the oldest victim-- taken at a carnival celebration at school, which showed her wearing large amounts of makeup--and presenting it as if this was how she normally looked, like some prostitute on the street. The headline above the frivolously, effectual picture said: *Lolita-murderer strikes again – Did she tempt her fate?* I wasn't the only one at the time who wondered how hey parents could have endured seeing their precious child being reported about in such a heartless and needlessly disrespectful manner.

And, suddenly as they'd begun, the murders stopped.

Because the murders had taken place far enough from our home, we were able to delude ourselves with a false sense of security, but there was one detail, one wish you made, which petrified me. The victims, shortly before their violent end, all colored their hair a blazing red. Beside the modus operandi and the juvenile age of the victims, this was the only characteristic present in all the cases assigned to the "Lolita Murderer." The victims visited neither the same school, nor the same association. They didn't live particularly near each other and appeared to have varied and often wildly different interests. How the perpetrator had made contact with them was unclear. When you told me to color my hair before our meeting and insisted it be blazing red, then I knew. I didn't want to believe it, much the way a wife denies her husband may be cheating, but I knew the truth. After you had determined my color of hair, more instructions followed. As if doing me a favor, you suggested we meet in Ferropolis at the concert of my favorite band, and then and there I would know who you were. As much I wished to be mistaken, I could only arrive at one conclusion. My stomach started to churn and I began to tremble uncontrollably. I shut down the laptop, ran into the hallway and tore the plug from the modem, as if this might lock you out of our lives for good. I needed time to cope with this new knowledge and clear my head. Three days later, I told you my mom had come into my room and taken my computer away because it was late and she wanted me to go to bed. *"I'm so sorry"*, I typed into the chat window. *"I don't want you to be angry with me."* A few seconds later your answer blinked across my monitor: *"Then I have a proposal for you."*

I can imagine what you're planning and what you're capable of. That I take as a tactical advantage. You, on the other hand, don't know who I really am, have no idea what I'm planning, and you surely don't anticipate the knife in my right boot. As I already said, the security checks were absolutely insufficient. Just like they usually are at such events.

The knowledge about your true nature has changed something in me. A conviction, which up to then seemed absolutely normal to me, had to be reconsidered. *You should not kill.*

Looks like you've made a profound thinker out of me. However, expect no thanks for it. Arriving at the *Gemini* I notice the stairs which lead upwards are blocked. A gigantic screen has been attached to the 200 foot-long interpreter, on which you can watch the show even better than on the stage itself. They have also blocked off about an eight-foot wide space in front of the stairs as an emergency corridor. A dreadful sight makes my blood freeze in my veins, just when I've reached this allegedly quiet place: Paramedics carry a young woman, covered in blood, on a stretcher along the path. A slender glass shard protrudes from her thigh, the jagged remains of a green bottle. Not brown, green.

Like her eyes. Those that stare at me while they roll her by. Then she opens her mouth and lets out a shrill, accusatory scream. The smell of iron is in the air. A young man runs beside her, shouting, "It was an accident! I didn't want to hurt you!" One of the security guards grabs his arm, pushes him aside, while the others rush by. Has he done this to her? His protestations of innocence involuntarily bring up the picture of my father in my mind's eye, even if he never seemed desperate after he had beaten up my mother. My look follows them, shattered. Still, I notice every detail that comes along with the scene. The horror dazes me and sharpens my senses at the same time. One of the stretcher's wheels causes a creaky noise. The injured girl is wearing the same sneakers a friend of my daughter owns as well. The band continues playing; the song's called *"The Kill"*. The howl of sirens interferes with the bass run. Three girls to my left whisper, one of them turns away and vomits, a few feet away people keep on dancing to the rhythm, and all I feel is the certainty that what I'm about to do is the right thing. Human beasts, men like you, have to be stopped. I've made myself familiar with the map of the area before I came here and know, if I turn right now and walk along the mighty jib crane, then I'll arrive at a small footpath, approximately 260 feet away from where I actually stand, which will lead me up to the *Big Wheel*. The first band's performance approaches its end and I look for a way past these little groups that still separate me from the path. Once certain no one is paying particular attention to me, I duck beneath the barrier tape, which is there to keep the hordes from the cultivated lawn between them and the illuminated steel monster. I take the cut through the grass, looking for shelter in the shadows of the vast *Gemini,* and walk to its other side. Normally this four hundred and ten foot long colossus is accessible for visitors, but not today. I am grateful that this backside area is mostly abandoned, because of the steely hulk and the attached canvas which blocks the view of the events onstage. I mustn't see, to know what's happening on the other side: The red sunset as well as the wildly starting applause let me know, that the main act is entering the stage, and that it's almost time.

My look falls on the scanty playground; a climbing frame and a gigantic sandpit, in which excavator miniatures are supposed to take the small museum visitors playfully back into the time of brown coal strip mining. Suddenly, I think of those sneakers again, which the injured girl wore, and of my children's hands, how they dug in the sand when they were younger. I remember how small and helpless they were when they were born, and the love I felt for them when I looked into their innocent eyes for the first time. How much they needed my protection.

In some ways, I feel very small and helpless in this moment myself. Should I see it as a remarkable coincidence that you want to screw me in range of a playground and kill me afterwards? Suddenly I sense the strip-mining giant looming overhead and threateningly darkened the sky. Fear takes hold in my gut, and for the first time since I came here, I begin to have doubts as to whether I can accomplish my task.

Of course I'd considered simply going to the police after finding out who it is I'm dealing with. But if I did, what then? If they caught you, you'd serve prison time but eventually you'd likely be freed. Did I want to spend my life fearing you might someday be on the loose again? Would you finish then, what you started now? Possibly you'd infest us once more. I also rated the risk, that my daughters' role in this game would push her into the center of the newsmakers attention. The sensation-mongering press would chew her up and spit her out again, probably tear her to pieces. Do I want to see pictures of my child in every pulpy magazine all over the country – maybe even those they'd find on your computer, the ones you used for threatening her, and a headline above that says *"This Lolita was supposed to be his next victim"*?

You've tried to turn someone beautiful into something filthy. You want to soil her, to throw her into the lake afterwards as if she were nothing but a piece of trash. Have you ever thought about anyone other than yourself in your entire life?

No, I dismissed going to the police again as an option. I'll help myself; will free myself of my fears and the world of you. I obsessed over this thought until you were so familiar that killing you seemed unavoidable. And now it's time to move, just like you, to the actual plan.

Chapter 5

Although the applause warns me, I wince when the music resumes and the band begins to play. I smile, recognizing the song, and regret I am unable to see the band, who in that strange moment seems to play for me alone. I square my shoulders and focus on the gigantic shovel wheel excavator enthroned on its chassis. In the slowly dying light, the steel giant contrasts with the sunset, sharp-edged and imposing. I take another deep breath, my rage growing as the music floats through the air. I walk and join in with the combat canto: *Someone call the ambulance, there's gonna be an accident. I'm coming up on Infrared, there is no running that can hide you, 'cause I can see in the dark …*

The fast bass line impels me, and in the end I'm almost running, now bound and determined again, up the hill, to the backside of the *Big Wheel*. Arriving there, I take shelter in the deep shadow of 1718 tons of steel, behind the twenty-six-foot-high conveyor. I try to steady myself, to calm my breath and to keep a lookout in all directions at once. From which direction will you come? My nerves are stretched to the breaking point, and my heart rate slowly returns to normal. For a moment I ask myself what I'm doing here. Waiting for death, done up like a dog's dinner? Something's for sure, neither my plan nor yours foresees that all participants will leave the crime scene alive. Who is going to play the killer? I'll stake everything to get it. The next song begins. The vocalists' melodic voice drifts through the night, and although it bolstered me before, it now asks doubtfully: *Baby, did you forget to take your meds?*

Maybe I should indeed let myself get medicated, best within the closed station of a psychiatric hospital, instead of being here and waiting for you. I must be crazy.

I start to freeze, although it's a warm midsummer evening. A cold shiver runs down my back. *"You need to call the police,"* whispers a voice inside me. *"You can't do this!"* I can't tell if its common sense or just fear.

I'm on the verge of turning around and leaving after all, but as it turns out, it's already too late. I hear your steps; the crunching of your heels in the slack gravel. Almost inaudible, thanks to the noise, but to me clearly discernible because of my overwrought senses. I freeze, inside and outside, and observe without a peep, how you take a look around. I melt into the night. The urge, to get away last second, is mighty. I overcome my stiffness; withdraw while you look in the other direction, a few steps farther, hiding even deeper in the shade of the steel giant. Now the gravel crunches under my boots. Your head turns in my direction. Your senses seem awake and sharpened too. The soft sounds caused by my attempted retreat catch your attention. You've detected my movement and seen me, your focus growing the closer to me you get. Still a few feet away, you stop, the weak shine of a single emergency light illuminating your face. You and your Facebook profile picture are identical. Your movements have lost everything juvenile and lanky and your true age is evident however. You certainly aren't in the beginning of your twenties. Unfortunately you look taller and firmer than I expected. Your voice is manly, very dark.

"Nice that you've come, you cute little mouse," I hear you say. "Come over here and let me take a look at you!"

The sound of your voice sends another chill

down my spine, because you sound so daunt-ingly normal. Reluctantly, I make a move out of the protective shade and step towards you. The fear in me grows with each step. My plan is to join in your play, to deceive you and to give you what you want, so I can overpower you while your trousers hang around your knees. I want to pull the knife from my boot and finally put you out of action when you least expect it. A straightforward plan that hasn't considered one thing: reality. I stop, yet outside your range. You're standing there with a confident smile, sizing me up.

"The new hair color looks amazing. Perfectly right for such a small, needy slut like you are! Now be a good girl and take off your top!"

If nothing else, I'm grateful you don't spend much time looking at my face, although it shocks me to see you move even faster at a real meeting than you do online. No hello, no careful approach.

"Hurry up!" Your tone is bossy and sounds satisfied at the same time; a mixture which fans the fury in me, while my knees start to tremble and feel a little weak at the same time.

I fiddle around with my top, cross my arms and grab the seam, raise it a little. While I take a few small steps backward, I pull it over my head and throw it to you. You try to catch it, but it falls to ground.

Slow, bad hand-eye-coordination, I note on my mental memo pad.

"Yes, that's good!" You praise me while you bridge this little distance, which I had regained, and reduce the gap between us.

"The bra too, you know what happens other-wise…" you whisper threateningly through the night. Quite close to me now, you reach for my breasts, knead them through the thin material, your hands rough and painful. Clumsily, I attempt to open my bra.

"Do I make you nervous, little bitch?" You grab me and pull me close to you. So close that I feel completely at your mercy. You're half a head bigger than me, and I feel your erection through the coarse material of your jeans, pressing at my belly. You rub your pelvis against me, turning yourself on.

"Can you feel that?" you ask with some sort of ridiculous pride in your voice. Suddenly you stop tormenting my breasts and grab my hair, hard.

50

The painful pulling causes me to follow the direction of your hand, and I kneel before you. The sharp pebbles press into my knees painfully as your free hand opens your belt then slowly unbuttons your trousers. At eye level, you present your measly weapon, which I assume is likely only fully operational when you level it at a vulnerable victim. My free hand gropes for my boots.

The beating hits me absolutely unprepared. I'd faint, if your hand didn't have such a lock on my head. Tears shoot into my eyes, blur my vision. For a split second I fear you've noticed what I'm up to, but as I see how the material of your underpants expands further, I understand that it's only about your enjoyment of power. The second strike hits my other cheek. Panic starts to grow. This is how my mother must have felt when my father was beating her. A part of me is afraid, almost scared to death, but another part, wild and strong, finds new strength.

You hold on to me and I force myself to remain calm, to not shout and to not defend myself. Tears run down my powdered cheeks, but not a single sound escapes from my mouth. Disobediently I stare up to you.

"Do you like him?" I remain quiet, but a disparaging smile pulls one corner of my mouth upwards, what you take as an occasion to repeat your question and to rub your genitals over my face. You take another swing, bitch-slapping me with strikes even more severe than those that came before. I don't know how many of these blows I can take, so it appears smarter to me to grant a demand.

With fragile voice I say: *"Yes."*

The musky, unwashed smell of your genitals causes a feeling of sickness in me.

I clear my throat and with a shaking voice say, "Yes, I like him!"

Does your clutch become a little looser?

"Can… can I see the whole thing?"

"Is that what you want?" Your voice tingles while you pull down your underpants. Do you really think a woman or a girl could feel desire for you under such circumstances? I need to be careful not to mistake your reaction for stupidity. It's all about making you believe your masturbatory fantasy is coming true now, so you'll let your guard down.

"Try it! It tastes like a lollipop."

"I love candy," I say, trying to look up at you while appearing as infatuated as possible. I try to lean back a bit so I can reach the leg of my right boot. Your voice becomes more aggressive again.

"Come on, I didn't take it out to air it."

You raise a hand, as if to strike me again, and I wince. Then you strike, slamming your fist against my face. "Or should I help?"

I don't have to try to sound scared when I ask you: "Can I touch it first?" But your brutality and your scorn don't only just frighten me; they function like an accelerant. Cold and calculating, I let my hand slide over your thigh, provocatively, rubbing you softly. I look up at you pleadingly, tears staining my face. "You don't have to hold me so tight. I'm here because I want to be. I want to nibble your lolli."

Your clutch loosens enough to give me hope.

"Please," I say, "may I touch it?"

My hand pets you, just inches from your crotch.

"He looks so big!"

Your sway must feel intoxicating in this very moment. You express your admiration for my humility with a contented, *"You little whore,"* and give me permission simultaneously.

First I stroke your cock real tender, then embrace him with my fingers and involuntarily think of those big naked snails that my granny divided with the spade whenever she found one in her garden. I'd like to do the same thing now. Instead I start jerking you off. With the free hand I feel for your small nuts, play with them a little. You moan. Your erection swells and your grip on me loosens even more.

"You're doing a real good job. Later I will give it to you too! Oh baby, I know, you'll like it

I double my efforts and adapt my movements to the rhythm of the music. Your moaning reminds me of the satisfied grunt of a pig. I'm disgusted and glad I'm wearing gloves. Finally, my efforts are rewarded, and you let go of my hair. With relish, too confidently, you cross your hands in the nape and demandingly stretch your pelvis towards me, as if there was nothing to be afraid of. I consider going for the knife, but leaning back at this point might make you suspicious, so I let your balls glide into the cup of my hand while the other keeps stroking you. I tear them out carefully – and squeeze them with all my strength. You roar like an animal, squirming with pain, and get caught in your lowered pants. You stumble but don't fall, already trying to pull up your pants. This gives me enough time to get on my feet. For a moment you are perplexed when I turn around and run to the two hundred foot long monument of steel; our room-divider behind which we hide from other people while we drop our masks.

The surprise doesn't last long. Your footfalls already pursue me. You're running after me, and I know at any long distance you'll have the advantage. Endurance has never been my strength. Unsure that I'll make it to the other side and the steps awaiting me there, I instead take the only other option I see, and throw myself into the arms of the shielding steel monster. I climb up onto one of the oversized teeth. I climb fast, without hesitation. Forcefully I move up, make my way hand over hand along one vast tooth after the other, until I reach the place at which the shovels of the earth-eating giant once threw the loamy food on a feeder band. I run along the dead conveyer belt, driven by your gasp behind me. Half way up I reach the stairs on which the maintenance staff ordinarily scales the hulk. I keep running, taking more than one rusty step at once. Fear and timid confidence are giving me stamina. Finally, I reach the summit and find myself at the top of the excavator, about thirty meters up. Wheezing, I stop and struggle to draw air into my lungs.

You're giving yourself some time, have slowed down your tempo. Maybe because you think that I sit in the trap up here. But now you've also arrived at the foot of the last stairs and stare up at me with a furious expression.

"In a jiffy I'll get you, you dumb little bitch!"

Did you speak those words aloud, or did I only hear them in my mind?

The last grain in the hourglass falls. Breathless and in a blind rage, like a bull in the arena, you climb the steps. Making the most of the height difference between us, I swing my leg and break your fast-approaching nose with a single, well-aimed kick, intensified by the steel cap in my boot.

A torrent of blood hurtles towards me like a red snake. You stumble back, step into nothing but emptiness, fall and find yourself at the foot of the stairs again. Numbly, you pick yourself up, a look of disbelieve on your face. You weren't prepared to be attacked. Maybe you didn't even expect any resistance. Although you slightly flounder, you're on your way up again; almost down too, because you slip on the rusty steps. That's why you master the rest of the climb on all fours, more crawling than rising, but still more than determined. You consist of hatred only – and this hatred totally blocks your vision.

Your hands arrive on top first, so ready to ultimately get me, that you overlook the knife that I pulled from my boot in the meantime. You're prepared for another kick, but not reacting fast enough when I squat down and ram something into your hand; cold metal that pierces the palm and pins it to the titan.

A shock could save you; prevent you from feeling the pain. But you're not simply pulling out the knife as if it were only a splinter; instead you're whining and congealing. Now I may not hesitate; if I want to keep the upper hand, I must act. Now! So I swing without mercy for an opponent who's already on the ground. Using my leg once more, my boot crashes against the side of your head and sends you into the land of dreams. You slump down with a grunt, giving me time to snap off the little key from my collar, which has always been the key for the handcuffs I wear as an accessory. I detach the jewelry in a hurry, and slap a cuff onto your wrist, closing the other around a segment of steel stairs, chaining you onto them. I reach for your other arm, drag with all my strength and turn you over onto your back. I bob up, but not before I restrain this wrist too. You lay before me, fixed, arms wide open.

At the same time, the music stops. In the short moment of silence, I gasp for breath. Briefly escaping death causes spontaneous euphoria. For the first time I recognize the breathtaking view that we have up here: Die illuminated steel monstrosities spring luminous into the starlit sky, spotlights sashay over the billowing heads of the viewers, light up an ocean of cluelessness. None of them lift their heads to see what's happening above them. An irritating fact underlining that I'm completely on my own. Small, like a ship's mast on the horizon, I see the shape of the lead singer onstage. Even at such distance I can see his face, larger than life and shining through the canvas attached to the *Gemini*. And I do almost believe he sees us too, because his plaintive voice so full of longing, seems to tell his listeners about your unpleasant situation, a song that tells of a servile, submissive man who crawls in the dust beneath the feet of his goddess.

Now it's me looking down on you. Helplessly, you lie there, unconscious and tied up. Your chest lifts and falls. I notice unaffected cold and factual, that every time you exhale, a bubble of blood balloons from your nostril. You belong to me entirely now, and finally, we're alone. You and I…and my blade.

I crouch down and grab the knife that's still stuck in your palm. I pull but it doesn't move. I crouch down, grab the knife, its blade still stuck in your palm, and attempt to pull it free. It doesn't move at all, seems to be anchored tightly. I grasp the knife with both hands and yank hard as I can and until it disengages. The blade leaves a bloody, gaping wound; stigmata that will scar you forever. The pain associated with it is bringing back your conscience, as your agonized moaning and your fluttering eyelids reveal. What's worse? Is it the pain in your head, the agony in your testicles or the ache in your palm?

Surprises me how great it feels to picture your pain, how much I enjoy seeing you bleed while you lay in front of me. I observe how you come to yourself. It takes a few seconds but you soon realize the predicament you're in. You try to move, notice how little elbowroom remains for your action, shake your chains in vain and flounder like a desperate beetle which a small, sadistic girl has turned on its back. Imbued with hatred, you stare at me, but on top of that I can see bewilderment and fear, which conjures a triumphant smile on my face. The moment I longed for has come. I ask myself whether you feel the same fear now which usually torments your victims. Are you afraid to die?

As if you'd heard the thought, you answer the unspoken question: "What do you want to do now, you silly cunt? Kill me? Well, go ahead then!"

I can tell from your tone that you're not yet convinced I'm capable of murder.

Soon, that will change.

Chapter 6

First of all you should learn to talk to me in another tone. Furiously I give your injured hand a kick and make you yell; a beautiful scream, but too loud.

Do I feel pity for you? No! An intoxicating mixture of fright and excitement takes place in me, causing a pleasant tingling. It feels good to give full scope to the hatred and the rage. Nevertheless, I must stem the risk that somebody could hear us.

"You should treat me with more respect," I lecture you in a calm but certain tone while I loosen the leather straps that are wrapped around my hip. I remove the yellow stress ball from my pocket.

"I'd even say you should treat women generally better than you do. But most of all you should leave your hands off little girls."

I suppress the desire to spit in your face, and instead bend down and press the knife to your throat. Not to slit, but to keep you from having bad ideas, like fighting back.

"Stay still or I'll cut you." I step over your bound arm and let myself fall astride your chest. I don't cushion my weight and you moan because the edges of the steps jab painfully into your back. Taking the knife away was a bad idea, as I've barely removed it when you try to throw me down and work against me with the untied legs, ramming your knees into my back. Like a rider on a stubborn horse, I raise the pressure of my thighs on your chest, strike out and hit you in the face with the knife-holding fist, before I put it to your throat again.

"Try that again and you're dead." You freeze immediately. The only thing that moves on you now is your face, contorted with pain. Your brain runs at full speed, just like mine. But the stupid thing is – I can see that too – you're capacities are already fully exhausted.

Not mine!

Look forward to suffer a fanciful repertoire of torture and pain, which I have pictured for myself at home, over and over! First, however, I must provide that you don't scream too loudly. The music makes it unlikely that someone below will hear us, but it seems wise, to play it safe and to dampen the yelling anyway.

"Open your mouth," I demand impatiently.

Pigheaded you keep it shut, so I position the blade directly under your right eye and repeat the instruction, menacingly calm: "Open your mouth! Now!"

This time you obey and open wide. I squeeze the soft anti-stress ball in, which I've mainly brought for this purpose.

"Just don't try any bullshit now. You better not kick or bite me! Or I'll provide for the fact that you won't see what I'm doing to you next." I move the knife aside, deposit it between my thighs on your chest. I need both hands. The threat seems to work. I take the wide, long leather tapes, my versatile belt substitute, tie them round your head and fix the ball in your mouth. I pull them so firmly that they cut in into your labial angles and knot them several times, after I've checked that the gag is jammed tight and can't slip.

Like a suckling pig, garnished with a lemon, you lie there.

While I take the knife up again, I ask myself whether it would feel the same to cut into your meat, as it feels to cut the Sunday roast. Momentarily I think about sliding deeper, to bore my knees harder into your thighs, so I'd have more comfort this time. "Shall I play with your cock again?" I whisper to you. "Would you like that? Come on... tell me you want me to fulfill my darkest and deepest desires!"

For this scenario I actually did some research; I was watching documentaries about the neutering of boars on YouTube.

The shoe fits, right? Your groaning a short while ago, when you were grunting like a pig, comes to my mind again and how you tried to make your toy tempting for me. In fact, castrating somebody doesn't seem to be so difficult, even the blood loss is nothing I worry about.

"Haven't you promised me a Lollipop? " I ask cold and venomous. "What are you going to do, if I simply go home now and take your sweets with me?" Are you fainting, or is it the cold light of the moon that makes your complexion suddenly appear unhealthy? I press the tip of the blade into the delicate skin beneath your jaw and move my face close to yours. So close, that in the vague light I can see every little wrinkle around your eyes. You can do nothing but stare at me as I push the sharp edged knife tip a bit deeper into your skin. A small drop of blood gushes forth, and I growl at you. "Hmm, what then?"

I recognize the fear in your eyes and my heart's racing, adrenaline rushing. Every muscle in my body is strained. The power I have over you has a mind-altering effect and brings a part of me to the light. Seeing how much you're shaking in your boots is something I really enjoy.

You'd probably like to answer me, however, the toggle prevents this and only a pitiful whimpering escapes from your throat.

"Haven't you promised you'd give it to me real good? " I ask with sweet poison in my voice. "Now it's probably the other way around." To see the fear in your eyes gives me a stouter feeling of satisfaction than your cock ever could.

A piercing smell penetrates my nose. You've peed in your pants like a baby. I could laugh, loud and satisfied, had the picture of another small child not pushed its way into my mind. I shake my head to expel this thought. You're not worthy of being compared to anything helpless or in need of protection. I rise up a little, decrease pressure on the blade and let it playfully wander over the contours of your neck. It glides about the collarbone and moves slowly deeper down to your chest. It comes to rest at the spot where other people but you have a heart. Of course I could grab the handle of the knife with both hands and stabbing down, find out if my suspicions are correct. Instead, I push your t-shirt up and glide with gloved fingers above your chest, because we're not done with the prelude yet. Your naked skin, covered in sweat, shimmers in the moonlight. Your quick breath lifts and lowers your chest, makes you look aroused, although you're only afraid. Now the blade caresses your nipples in circles. You're struggling with your feet, trying to fight back somehow, and hit my back again.

This hurt!

You deserve what comes now. Resolutely I apply more pressure on the knife, let its grin cut through your skin and sink into the flesh of your breast, just a little. The stammering sounds become a suppressed shout.

"That's because you didn't keep still. You need to be more careful, otherwise you might hurt yourself."

I need to hold on to the rage that still seethes in me, because seeing your wound and the frightened look on your face causes more than a feeling of elation: For the first time you don't only appear to me as a monster or the personification of evil, but human. I feel cold, because I recognize that it really wasn't harder for me to cut you, than to carve a Sunday roast. Were I to look in a mirror, would the same monster I found in you stare back at me? The feelings of power and satisfaction aren't as pure as they were before I realized your humanity.

I slide deeper between your legs, kneeling once more at the height of your genitals. Meanwhile, I can smell your fear; this smell has nothing to do with the wet spot on your trousers, however. You exhale it. It's creeping out of your pores.

Only few handles would be needed to bare you, so the most sensitive parts would lie defenselessly and blank before me. Your suppressed whining becomes pure, reaches panic level when I press the tip of the knife where your pathetic little worm tries to creep away into your groin.

"Shut up! I can't stand your whining. It makes me wanna hurt you!"

You obey immediately. Fascinating how submissive you can be. I hope you appreciate my dominance as well, which plays out fully now, when I compliment you:

"Yes, that's good! What do you think, should I help you become a real brave little girl? "

I drop a hint, let the knife glide over your groin area and enjoy that you start shaking beneath me, totally out of control. My look falls on the bulge in your trousers that now stands out, since the erection that distracted attention away from it is missing; time to see what you carry with you. Gingerly I pick out a prepaid cell and... the garrote you've used to strangle your innocent victims. My hands aren't shaking when I swing it in front of your face like a Foucault pendulum.

You think the time has come: Now I'm gonna cut off your balls first, then I'll take your life with your own murderous instrument. And there's nothing you can do about it. That's for sure. Blank dismay, absolute helplessness and fear of death are reflected in your face again – and I let my grin solidify; wipe it off. I've seen this expression before. It lay on the face of my mother.

One of my first memories is the sight of my father, as he knelt over her, his hands firmly closing around her throat. Back then the same fear of death lay in her eyes I can see now in yours. I remember leaping at him, drumming at his back with my small fists, so he would let her go.

Now I can't suppress my own shaking anymore. No matter what you did or will do, that doesn't make it right that I'm going to become a perpetrator too. The fear of you and the hatred you cause in me were clouding my sight, but now something in me straightens out, makes me stand up and step back in a hurry. A wave of nausea and disgust overruns me: I'm disgusted by you, by me and most of all by what I almost did. Best I'd like to turn around, to run down the steps and into the lake which embraces the city of steel. Dive into it and wash your smell, your touch, your stinking blood and the guilt off me, with cold, clear water. But I know, first I must do something else. One last time I bend to you and look into your face; differently than before, compassionately and at the same time horrified. My sad look is telling you about my anger and fury, it reveals my age, shows how much you were wrong about me and it is letting you know, that you've lost. Additionally there's something else you can see: You and me, we're not the same. I surely could take somebody else's life, I just don't want to. Not anymore. But that's no reason for you to feel relieved. This won't be over quickly for you.

"Tell them the key is somewhere down there," I say and drop the key for the handcuffs through the grids of the stairs. I hear it hitting ground. I pocket your cell, taking the portable evidence with me. I put the garrote down, beyond your reach. The police will surely show a lot of interest in this object.

I'll never again be afraid of you. You won't hurt me or my loved ones ever again. I've won! Now, because I feel no more fear, I don't want to commit a murder. Rather, I'd like to give you a gift. Your life, how you've known and led it up to now, will be changed by me. Possibly it will alter my life as well and affect the lives of my children. I'm quite sure the police will find out what has happened here tonight and which role I played in this game. And maybe a press pack will camp in front of my door. However, I also have no more fear facing this. I've defeated you, and that gives me the feeling I'd be able to master simply anything. No matter what comes, we can handle it.

I drop the knife.

It doesn't take long for the police to arrive at the scene. Bright floodlights cut through the night and the darkness that surrounds you. From a distance, standing in cold water that reaches up to my knees, I observe how they carry you away; into a new world of steel, with iron curtains before your windows.

Author's Note

My heartfelt thanks go out to the people who were essentially involved in the process of making this book. Without you I never would have made it so far.

Most of all I thank Greg F. Gifune for his great work editing my translation. I'm sure it wasn't easy at all times, to figure out what the german girl wanted to say.

Last but not least I want to thank my family for their support, and my german publisher, dotbooks. And, of course, thanks to the great REDRUM-Team, that supports me.

The Favorite Girl

BONUS STORY by Simone Trojahn

He sipped from his whiskey, couldn't keep his eyes off her.

What a woman! Fucking hell!

The thick blonde mane almost reached her ass.

And that was some ass! My God!

Plump and heart-shaped. Something to touch. Or bite.

And she'd packed it into these incredibly tight jeans!

If he'd given a fuck about Christmas or birthdays, that would probably have been the gift he wished for …

John licked his lips.

A lump formed in his throat that no whiskey in the world could flush down.

His jeans slowly became too tight.

He scratched his crotch and drank. His greedy eyes remained on the woman. They were gliding over her taut body like slugs.

And she just sat there. Straight as a pole. A glass of wine stood in front of her. She wore these brazenly tight pants and a short red top.

Red! Goddamn!

And she was alone.

Wasn't she in the mood for some company?

What was a girl like that doing in a fucked-up bar like this? Weekdays and after midnight?

Who was she and what did she have in mind?

Usually there were only workers from the nearby factory here. They drowned their after work worries in booze, and on weekends one or the other bitch came here in search of a quick fuck.

Cheap sluts with fat asses and too much makeup in their swollen faces.

John was one of the guys who worked in the factory, and not a day went by without him wondering if that had been everything already …

He approached his forties and had been divorced for two years now.

His two daughters were now teenagers and only talked to him when they needed money. His ex had a new stud who didn't seem to mind her wobbly thighs and the wrinkles around her eyes.

She'd been beautiful.

And horny!

John had forgotten when that was.

Today she was a ridiculous fat cow who pestered him about alimony payments. The kids were in college now. And who had to pay for that?

John seldom thought of his daughters or the past. They had been cute pudgy girls with cute pigtails and round eyes. They had adored their daddy. And he would have done anything for them.

Anything!

Now they were bimbos with garish makeup and bleached hair who didn't give a shit about their daddy.

As long as he gave them enough money.

And he did, as long as he was working himself to death at the factory.

What had become of his family?

They had been happy once.

Or …?

Nowadays John had a beer belly and too much fat on his hips, his chest was already wobbling, his beard was gray, and his hair would follow soon.

He spent the evenings here, drinking whiskey to ease the pain in his back … and to forget.

Tomorrow morning at six he would have to struggle his way out of bed again, stretch his stiff limbs, and try to cover the disgusting taste in his mouth with toothpaste.

He'd drink liters of black coffee and smoke one cigarette after the other, get into his old pickup and drive to work, thinking of the evening, the bar, the next whiskey.

That's what he was living for now.

There was nothing else for John anymore.

While staring at the blonde woman (and he wasn't the only one to do so), he wondered when he'd last seen a pussy up close.

Months ago.

And the pussy in question hadn't necessarily been what a man in the prime of his life was longing for after a hard day's work.

Its sour and fishy smell had expanded John's limit of disgust by a few nuances.

He'd fucked the slut nonetheless.

You didn't always have a choice.

He wondered how this pussy would smell?

And taste?

Even the thought of it made John breathless.

It would be sweet. And juicy.

What was that girl doing here?

He couldn't stop asking himself this question.

If she were his daughter …

But she ain't, man! And you should thank God for that.

Had she come to make him lose his mind?

His colleagues apparently had the same problem.

Even the bartender had an expression on his face that seemed horny and transfigured.

The woman surely knew all eyes were on her. It didn't seem to bother her. Maybe she even liked it. Why else would she be sitting in such a bar at this hour?

She's waiting for it! John thought in his heated skull. *If you don't seize the opportunity, someone else will.*

But who?

He was by far the youngest and (as far as John could judge) the most attractive man in this bar.

After all, there had to be a reason why the sluts loved to throw themselves at him!

He was nothing special and had long since passed his best days, but he was still the best piece of man this sad honky-tonk had to offer.

Would the woman think the same?

Didn't she look over at him a few minutes ago? Hadn't she winked at him?

Why don't you try your luck?

That was a good question. What did he have to lose?

If she was here to seriously pick up a guy, she was eventually just a slut and he should have felt sorry for her …

Why wouldn't he take advantage of the situation?

In a life that no longer had much to offer, that was a very special treat.

To refuse it wouldn't only be stupid but almost a sin.

So John took his glass and walked over to the woman who was still sitting stiff and silent on her bar stool.

When he stood next to her, he could smell her.

Her perfume was too tangy for his taste, but a look into her neckline simply compensated for everything.

"Hi!" he murmured and raised his glass. "I'm John."

"Hi!" Her voice sounded deeper than expected. A little hoarse and damned wicked.

John's cock wanted to dance.

She closed her long fingers with the red lacquered nails around the stem of the wine glass.

Red!

"Cheers!" she whispered. A soft smile played around her full lips.

"Cheers!"

They drank without taking their eyes off each other.

"What's your name?"

She batted her eyelashes that were too thick to be real.

"Angel."

John suspected that was a lie, but he didn't care.

His gaze was trapped in her neckline.

At the rosy edge of her nipples!

Good Lord, she really was an angel!

Their glasses were empty and John was happy to provide supplies.

He ignored the bartender's disparaging gaze. That guy was just jealous!

Angel's deep blue eyes drilled into his.

John imagined kissing her sweet little snub nose. And these lips ...

She was hardly any older than his daughters, but that didn't matter.

"Where you from, Angel?"

The answer was obvious. This wonderful being must have fallen from heaven ...

"I'm not from around here," she whispered.

Was there and bit of sadness in her voice?

"Passing through?" John had noticed a black travel bag standing next to her on the floor.

She shrugged. "Something like that."

John was satisfied with that information. After all, he wasn't a psychiatrist or social worker, just a horny guy with a hard cock!

"Do you know where you're sleeping to-night?"

Again she shrugged.

Bingo! Surely she didn't have any money! She was probably running away from something or someone; she was helpless and on her own.

It couldn't be any better for him!

I'll fuck you tonight, baby!

"You can come with me if you want."

She looked at him and seemed to think about it. She frowned and played with a strand of her long hair.

Finally, her face brightened. She grinned and suddenly looked like a twelve-year-old. "Sure! Why not?"

John grinned too. He had every reason to. "Then let's get outta here!" he hastily suggested.

He'd forgotten his morning shift and the fat on his hips.

He'd forgotten all his worries and doubts.

For tonight, an angel had fallen from heaven.

***

On the way to the parking lot, John carried Angel's bag, which was surprisingly light.

He wondered if she was really on the run.

On high heels? Only with a small bag and a thin leather jacket?

Or maybe she was just a traveler looking for happiness and for a real good man?

Well, she found him now, John thought and smiled.

Who cared anyway?

The looks of the other men had been worth their weight in gold when they left the bar together.

His angel.

John had deserved that.

After all these years of deprivation between flabby thighs and fishy pussies.

He stared at Angel's ass.

How her ass cheeks bobbed …

John already saw himself grabbing between them and pulling them apart. A sweet little revelation. He'd stick his tongue in first and then maybe a finger. He'd …

They had arrived at his pickup.

John wanted to touch Angel. No matter where. Right now!

He reached out and helped her get in the truck.

Angel gave a dreamlike, sweet smile.

She was a real piece of candy!

Oh man, he'd fuck her brains out …

John was dizzy with happiness when he started the engine.

Now she was sitting right beside him, filling
the stale smell of his car with a fresh scent.

His angel.

John set off.

Ten minutes.

He would have liked to drive even faster.

Too risky.

He pulled himself together but still could only
think of his throbbing cock and Angel's pretty
little butthole. Most girls didn't like it when you
took the back door, but John didn't care about
that.

Not tonight.

***

The stinking old skank that John had fucked last
had been up for anything. Even today, he still
shuddered when he thought of her worn-out
holes and wrinkled grayish skin. Nevertheless,
he'd kept her for a few days before he chased
her away, for his cock was by no means as picky
as he was.

He to admit that her blowjobs had been pretty
good.

And it was a good thing having a woman in your apartment when you came home after a long day at work. John had canceled a few evenings in the bar to enjoy her macaroni with cheese instead. Together they had eaten, drunk, smoked and most of all fucked their brains out.

If only she'd been a little younger and prettier …

In the end, John got tired of her.

What would it be like with Angel?

He could well imagine keeping her forever. She could cook for him and massage his cock. She could clean the apartment and let him fuck her ass.

Every night.

Then it would finally make sense again to struggle yourself out of bed in the morning and drag your aching carcass to the factory. The thoughts of Angel would sweeten John's days and turn his nights into fireworks. He'd never have to go to a bar again to get pointlessly drunk.

But Angel was so beautiful … so young …

Whoever or whatever had driven her into his arms tonight, she certainly wouldn't want to stay.

Absolutely not!

What's a girl like her supposed to do with a guy like him?

It was crazy to imagine that at all.

Completely crazy!

Although … she wasn't a local. Nobody knew her. And she was already making quite a secret of herself, which probably suggested that she sure had a skeleton in the closet or at least something to hide.

Girls like her were rarely missed.

His colleagues and the bartender had seen her leaving the bar with him, but was that of any importance? They would believe him if he claimed she'd left him the next day.

Why not?

They must have thought she was a hooker anyway.

What pretty young woman would wear a provocative outfit to sit in a bar full of horny factory workers?

And she'd left with John without batting an eye, even though he was a stranger.

What decent girl would do that?

She was either totally desperate or just as horny as he was.

Only that she could have picked better guys than old Johnny, who had to make an effort to see his dick while peeing.

Well, he'd make a special effort to make her happy tonight.

He'd do his very best for his Angel.

Even if it was the last thing he did, ha-ha!

She now sat on John's worn-out couch, her long slender legs crossed, a glass of whiskey in her hand.

John had put on music (Aerosmith, good old-fashioned shit) and dimmed the lights. His pants got tighter when he sat next to Angel.

It had to be clear to her that this was about sex, but she smiled sweetly and seemed very relaxed.

Because she wanted it too or because she didn't know what he was up to?

Well, we'll find out pretty soon.

John put his glass down and bent over her. Her mouth tasted of whiskey and was sticky from her lip gloss. She returned John's kiss and didn't fight back when he grabbed her breasts.

Everything was perfect!

But the world was spinning a little too fast.

Had he drunk that much?

John grabbed Angel by the wrist and led her hand to his crotch.

She massaged him.

Ah, good, that was so awesome!

He tugged at her top, tore it down, and freed her big breasts.

Great! Those nipples!

John sucked on them like a toddler.

Too bad he got a little nauseous now.

Maybe he shouldn't have eaten yesterday's burger for lunch today after all.

But damn, that felt so hot!

Was his zipper open already?

All of a sudden, Angel's hand was deep in his pants.

John greedily sucked on her nipples, her neck, her mouth …

Or was it her chin?

He could no longer see clearly, and his sense of touch seemed to have left him.

Damn booze!

That had to stop!

Angel covered his face with wet kisses.

Her tangy scent turned John on.

He lifted his hands to grab her, wanted to push her down and turn her around, take off his pants, knead her ass …

But his limbs were suddenly so heavy …

John moaned.

The sounds he made ranged from lust to pain.

What was she doing with his dick?

That hurt!

Fuck!

He wanted to push her away but instead slumped down like a wet sack.

What the fuck?

What was she doing with him?

Why did that hurt so much?

He tried to yell at her, but instead of words, a gush of vomit came out of his mouth. At least that made her let him go.

John wanted to look at her, talk to her.

Her face was blurred.

Not an angel anymore.

He felt a burning pain in his crotch.

What had she done?

He wanted to get up, grab her, beat the shit out of her, and then fuck her soul out of her body …

He couldn't. He seemed paralyzed.

All he could do was puke.

What had she given him?

Poison? Drugs?

What did angels bring from heaven?

John couldn't think anymore.

The pain pulsated red in his brain.

Red.

Shadows twitched before his eyes.

And somewhere in the background Steven Tyler was singing, "And then at times I'm so weak from lovin', I couldn't even carry a tune …"

John was weak too. Just not from making love. Or was it somehow …?

Take me with you! John thought desperately. *Get me outta here!*

But Steven didn't even think about it.

Nor did anybody else.

***

When John regained consciousness, it was cold and quiet.

He looked down at himself and realized he was naked.

His penis and testicles pulsated painfully.

Angel had used shoelaces (presumably his own) to bind his genitals into a grotesque object. The skin was bluish and swollen where the blood was accumulating. It felt as if it would burst open at any moment.

Please don't! Dear God! Please, please don't!

The pain was terrible.

Compared to that, the whirring in John's head and the tingling in his tied limbs felt almost pleasant.

Angel had dragged him from the couch to the floor and tied him up there. John could see duct tape (probably from his kitchen) on his ankles. She must have also used it to tie his hands behind his back.

"Angel?" he croaked hoarsely. "Where are you? Angel?! Damn fucking bitch!"

He couldn't see her.

That fucking slut!

She was completely crazy!

This was kidnapping!

And torture!

What was that bitch thinking?

"Angel?! Please, let … let's talk about it! Hear me? *Angel!*"

Considering what that bitch had done to him, her name was pure mockery.

Now John was sure this wasn't really her name.

That miserable whore!

Had she planned this from the beginning?

Probably!

Now it made sense.

John wriggled in his shackles and threw his head back and forth, which only made him nauseous again.

Don't vomit! Not again!

He retched dry. Nothing happened.

Again he screamed her name.

Angel! This damn spawn of hell!

Maybe she was long gone. And maybe that was the best thing that could happen to him. He'd have enough time to free himself. And if he didn't manage that, sooner or later someone from work would come by to check on him. An embarrassing situation, for sure, but still better than to die here, killed by this devilish woman …

And what if my dick rots off by then?

John had no idea if that was anatomically possible. He didn't know anything about such things. But the thought scared the shit out of him.

Could he lose his cock?

Or his virility?

Again he fought against the shackles, but the tape wouldn't move an inch.

In any case, he hadn't bought any shit!

Even if he now wished he'd …

"Angel!"

Did he really want her to still be here?

Maybe she wasn't finished with him yet …

On the other hand, he might be able to talk to her and convince her to let him go.

She was just a stupid bitch! How hard could it be?

"Angel? Please talk to me if you' re here! Don't leave me like that!"

And then she actually showed up.

The long hair framed her face and added a deceptive softness to her features. She was naked and she moved with the gracefulness of a Greek goddess.

Angel.

John almost didn't notice the carving knife in her hand.

She'd taken it from his kitchen.

Just like the tape.

Angel came closer.

John panted breathlessly. He'd be hyperventilating in a minute. Desperately, he tried to free his hands. Panic and nausea raged in his guts, stealing his breath. He knew exactly how well this damn knife could cut! He'd sharpened it only a few days ago.

Dear God, you can't let that happen!

But why not?

What would he have done to that woman if he could?

Did someone like him really deserve mercy?

Even now, with all the panic and pain, he was still gawking between Angel's legs.

She was shaved.

"P-please!" he stammered as she squatted next to him. "Don't hurt me!"

Tears ran down his cheeks now. He hadn't even cried at his father's funeral five years ago.

Angel's hair hung down to his upper body.

Like gold.

Then she grabbed his crotch and John screamed in pain.

"Is that good, Johnny? Pretty tight?" She didn't sound mocking but strangely serious.

"Take it away!" John whimpered. "Please, remove it!"

Angel smiled and squeezed again.

John roared until everything turned black before his eyes.

Finally she let go.

"Please, Angel, let me go!"

"But where do you wanna go, you sad old man?"

She lifted the knife, turned it around, looked at it from all sides. Finally she stuck it tip first into John's belly button.

A stabbing pain shot through his abdomen.

Angel grabbed the handle with both hands and slowly turned the knife.

John felt the blade drill into his flesh. He tried to pull in his stomach and hold his breath. "Stop it! Please!"

But Angel didn't stop. She leaned all her weight on the knife, which finally disappeared up to the handle in John's belly with a smacking noise.

The pain was as sharp and pointed as the cursed blade that John had sharpened himself.

He felt warm moisture and knew it was his blood.

Red! Red like her fingernails.

He gasped and stared at Angel's rocking breasts. Her flowing hair glided over his skin.

She let the knife stick in John's belly and beamed at him.

This smile made the sun rise.

John would have given anything to wake up next to this girl only once in the morning.

After a long night of happiness and sex.

But that wasn't the reason she was here for …

"Soon you'll have it done," she whispered.

"W-why are you doing this to me?"

Angel's bright white teeth flashed when she laughed.

"'Cause you're one of them, my darling."

"Who are you talking about?" John shook his head. "You're wrong!"

The warm liquid spread, running over his chest and thighs.

The pain was even bearable.

For the moment.

She straightened up. Only now did he notice the scars on her otherwise flawless body. There were a lot of them in the pubic area.

"Who hurt you?"

Angel just smiled.

"Angel, please! I can help you!"

"You're dying, Johnny. That's all that's left for you to do in this life."

"Tell me who hurt you! We can go to the police, we—"

"I was his favorite girl." Suddenly her voice sounded younger. "His princess."

She sighed. Her gaze drifted into nowhere. Lost in thought she played with her breasts. Her fingers were stained with blood.

His blood.

Red!

"But he couldn't save me either. Nobody can."

"But I can, Angel! Please believe me!"

"He's dead now. They're all dead. And I'm still their favorite girl."

"Please, Angel, listen to me! You have to pull the knife out of my stomach! Very carefully! And then …"

Angel massaged her nipple with one hand while the other slipped into her shaved crotch.

Her lips formed an O.

John thought of the women in the sex commercials who apparently brought themselves to orgasm with their own fingers.

A typical male fantasy.

But this was nothing but a nightmare that had come alive!

Whatever that girl had experienced, she was crazier than a shithouse rat and he was so fucked!

Angel moaned and pushed her pelvis forward.

Suddenly she paused and stared right in John's face. Smiling, she reached for the knife in his stomach.

John flinched, trying to prepare for the pain. No important organs seemed to be injured yet, although the blade stuck deep inside his body.

"You would have love to fuck your favorite girl, right?"

John's mind was spinning.

What should he say?

What was the right thing to do?

Was there even a right or wrong?

Angel slowly moved the knife handle back and forth. The pain intensified.

John tried to be strong. He knew this was his last chance.

"Y-you're a pretty woman, Angel. Beautiful. And I admit that I wanted to sleep with you. What man wouldn't? But I … I'd never have hurt you. Do you understand? Never! I just wanted to be tender and—"

"You would have fucked me hard, right, old man?"

"No!" John sobbed. "I would have been very tender."

"Oh, tender?" Her face distorted into a grimace as she grabbed the knife and shoved it up to John's sternum.

He felt his flesh gape apart, and he screamed his head off.

Angel now looked like a fury gone wild, speckled with his blood.

Red!

She left the knife stuck, turned around, and held her ass in front of his face. "That's what you wanted, right?"

John fought for his consciousness. He opened his eyes and stared at Angel's scarred flesh. God alone knew what had happened to this woman.

If she hadn't just slit his tummy open, he might have had the chance to think about it a little more. But all he could do was moan and whine for mercy. He only subconsciously realized she was peeing in his open abdominal cavity and that her hands were now stuck deep in his gaping wound.

John looked into her sparkling eyes and saw bliss.

Black dots danced in front of his field of vision.

His body shook violently as Angel rummaged in his guts.

Suddenly he remembered his daughters, whom he'd never see again.

"I have kids!" he rasped with his last strength.

Angel had just pulled a bowel loop out of his abdominal cavity and wrapped it around her wrist like a grotesque bracelet. It stank of blood, fear, and excrement.

John's innards were glued to Angel's body, which had been badly battered by life.

And again she plunged very deeply into him, dug up to the elbows in his guts, tore and pulled …

John's heart rate slowed. He could no longer lift his head, and it took great effort to keep his eyes open.

His younger daughter Jennifer had been his favorite. Angel could have been. He only would've hurt her a little.

Not as bad as the men whose darling she'd been before.

But it was too late for all that now.

Angel looked like a monster, full of blood, slime, and shit.

A favorite girl to run away from.

An angel from hell.

John's tied hands twitched behind his back, looking for a hold they wouldn't find anymore.

Angel's delicate fingers squished his pancreas. That hardly hurt.

John's last thought was that he probably deserved it.

He wasn't any better than all the others …

But in the end, it wasn't him sticking in her but her sticking in him and maybe he still had a bit of luck, because he was allowed to look at those beautiful golden hairs and those pretty big tits until the end, which trembled to the beat of her lust.

And this one promise she gave him on his way into the darkness: she'd be his favorite girl.

Forever.

PUBLISHING PROGRAM

www.redrum-verlag.de

1. Bad Family: *Simone Trojahn*
2. Selina´s Way: *Simone Trojahn*
3. Basement Games: *Simone Trojahn*
4. He´s Angry: *Moe Teratos*
5. Cannibal Hilidays – The Beginning: *Ralph D. Chains*
6. Fida: Stefanie Maucher

REDRUM CUTS

1. Witch Juice: *Simone Trojahn*
2. Bizarre: *Baukowski*
3. Ferropolis: *Stefanie Maucher*

STEFANIE MAUCHER

FIDA

THRILLER

REDRUM

Fida

What would you do if your child just disappeared? If you don't know if it's still alive or dead? Would your family grow closer together or break under the load?

At what point would you give up hope? And how far would you go if you found the culprit?

Thirteen-year-old Laura didn't come home after visiting the library. The police quickly found a suspect – but no trace of the girl. Tatjana has been searching for her daughter for more than a year and isn't willing to give up hope …

Tom always wanted a pet. Preferably a puppy that obeys his commands. But at that time his father already knew about Tom's vicious, sadistic drives and so the wish for a toy remained unfulfilled for a long time. To this day! Because Tom is grown up now and he thinks it's time to fulfill his wishes by himself. Time for Fida!

Vincent Prize 2013 awarded in the category of 'Best German Novel'.

'FIDA' is the author's first book published by REDRUM BOOKS.

REDRUM

SIMONE TROJAHN

THRILLER

BASEMENT GAMES

Basement Games

Karl is shocked when Toni kidnaps a young woman to keep her imprisoned in the basement of their house. His brother is a sadist. He's always been.

Karl is torn between pity, emotional dependence on his brother, and the need to satisfy his own urges on pretty Laura, who sees in him the only hope of rescue.

Will Karl do the right thing and help the girl escape, or will his dark side prevail?

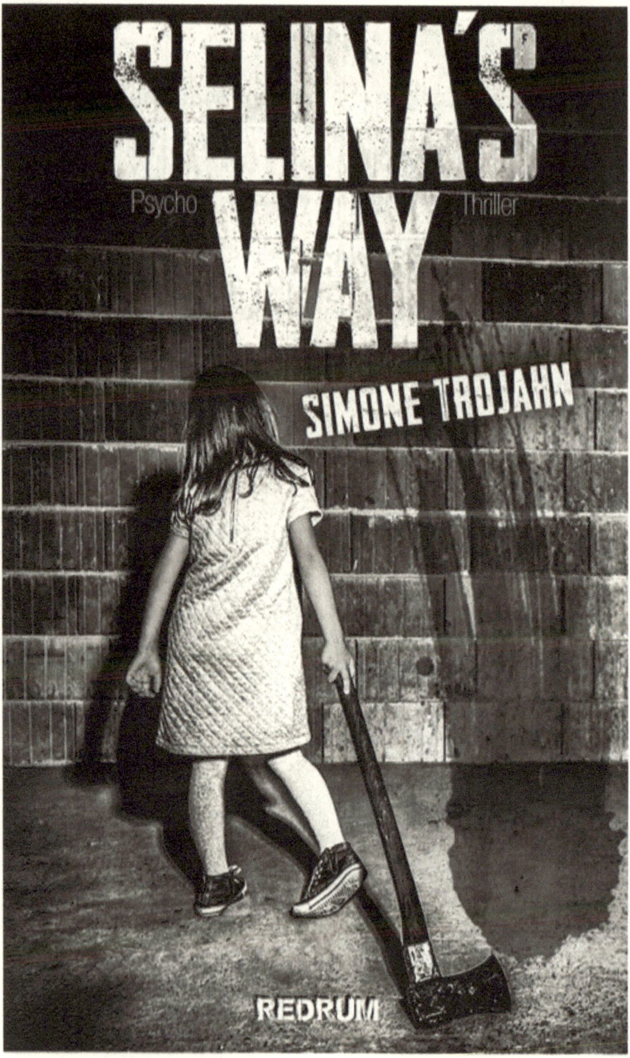
SELINA'S
Psycho
WAY
Thriller
SIMONE TROJAHN
REDRUM

Selina´s Way

Do you have kids? Do you love them? Would you do anything for them?

Really anything?

Dan Meller once lived in a rundown trailer park. He was an alcoholic, addicted to drugs, and barely able to look after his little daughter, Selina.

Today, Dan is clean and sober and seems to have made it. Together with his wife and two daughters, he lives in a pretty house on the outskirts of town, has a job, and only has the best intentions.

The little girl from back then is now almost an adult. A pretty young woman.

Daddy's pride and joy.

And of course he does everything to make up for what he screwed up in the first years of her life.

But Selina looks at things a little differently.

A dark abyss hides behind her radiant façade, because deep in her broken soul, she is still a neglected toddler.

She needs her daddy so much!

And Dan will do anything to make his beloved daughter happy.

Really anything!

You don't want this girl to be your enemy!

SIMONE TROJAHN

BAD FAMILY

THRILLER

REDRUM

Bad Family

What does family mean to you? Warmth, security, solidarity?

Then you haven't yet met the Kollers …

Seventeen-year-old Fips and his siblings have hard-ly known what a normal family is. Living with a sa-distic father and an insensitive mother is a nightmare of oppression and violence.

Through the years, the domineering head of the family has succeeded in completely instrumentalizing his own family and degrading his children to hench-men of his cruel crimes.

Fips also commits unspeakable atrocities under his father's guidance. By the time he finally finds the strength to fight his demons, time is running out. Will the boy succeed in saving his father's victims as well as his own soul, or is it already too late?.

SIMONE TROJAHN

WITCH JUICE

REDRUM
HORROR - CUTS

Witch Juice

A small collection of short stories for readers of extreme literature. But beware: The descent into the abysses of the human mind is at one's own risk.

It includes stories by Germany's most disturbing horror and thriller author Simone Trojahn and the Queen of Madness: A.C. Hurts.

More than 100,000 enthusiastic readers. Without exception, all of Simone Trojahn's books can be found in the German Amazon Top 20 or in the Top 10 Thriller & Horror Charts.

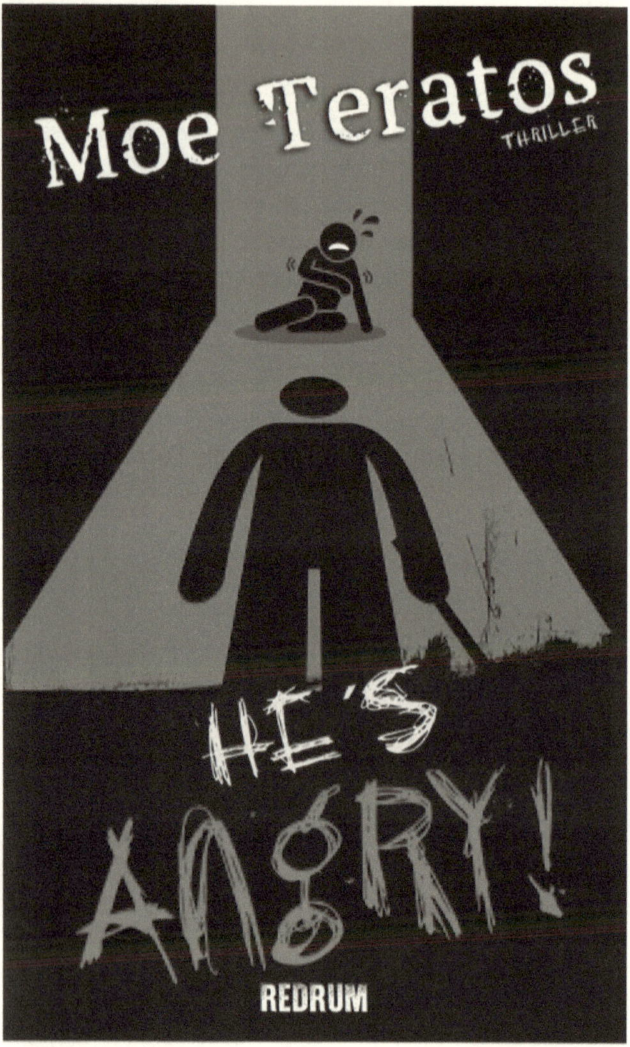
Moe Teratos
THRILLER
HE'S
ANGRY!
REDRUM

He´s Angry

Anton is shy and never had a girlfriend yet. But like everyone else, he has needs and one day he learns to satisfy them in a brutal manner. It's the ultimate insight for him - but the biggest nightmare for the women who meet him. Especially for Annabella and her friend Frida, who are soon imprisoned and tortured in Anton's house.

REDRUM
HORROR
RALPH D. CHAINS
CANNIBAL HOLIDAYS
THE BEGINNING

Cannibal Holidays – The Beginning

Germany's hardcore author number 1!

At the low point of his life, Peter Logan discovers the ad: "Travel with us to experience the last cannibals." It turns out to be a wild trip with a group of fetishists whose biggest desire is to be reduced to meat by cannibals. Once in the jungle, the cruel reality surpasses their most perverse fantasies by far. Sex, drugs, and violence fascinate Peter, and he experiences a journey that goes beyond any limits and answers the question of what remains at the end of life. Not an immortal soul, but only bones and cannibal excrements.

REDRUM loves you!

REDRUM liebt dich!

Visit our facebook group now: .

REDRUM BOOKS - Nichts für Pussys!

www.redrum-verlag.de

www.ingramcontent.com/pod-product-compliance
Lightning Source LLC
Chambersburg PA
CBHW021119130626
46554CB00002B/776